Arab dhow

Chinese junk

Kayak (modern)

Coxed eight-person
racing scull

The *Victory*—Lord Nelson's flagship

This boat pulls other boats.

This boat has many lights.

This boat carries planes.

This boat pulls people.

This boat brings help.

Raise the gangplanks! Hoist the anchor!

This boat has one large light.

This boat needs help.

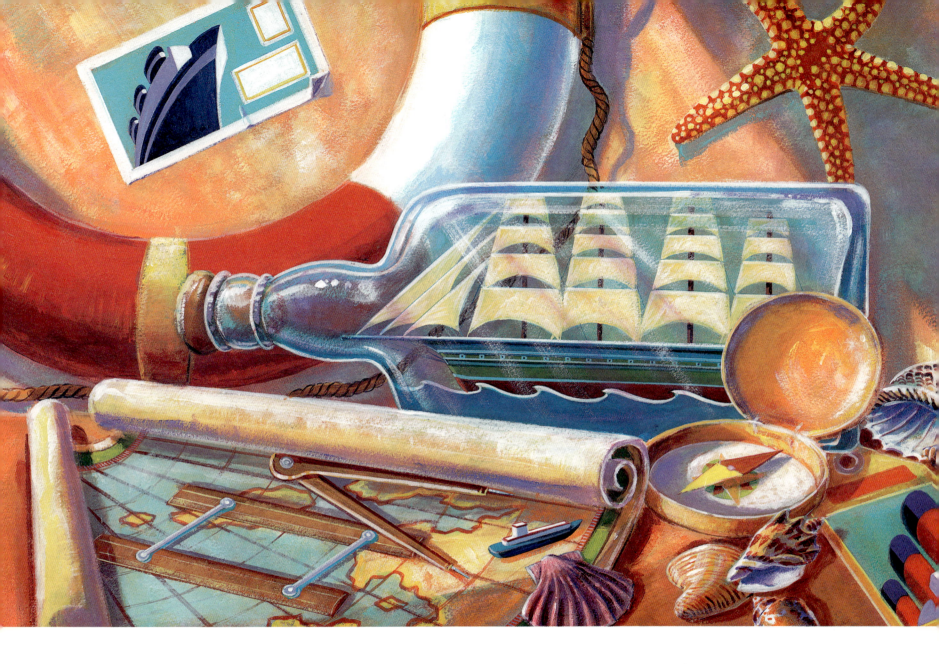

This boat is in a bottle.

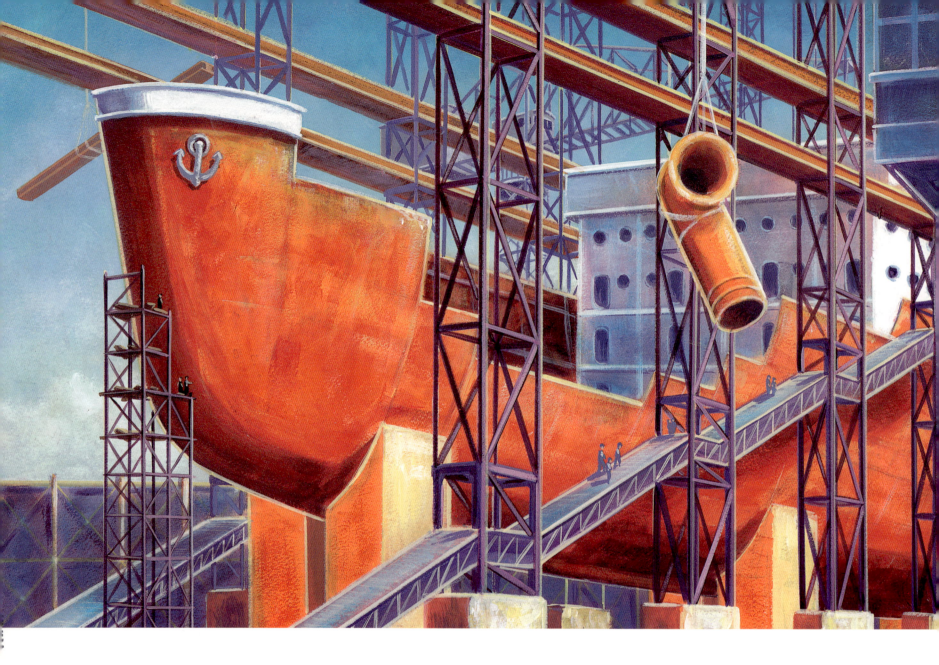

This boat is being made.

This boat is being launched.

This boat is made from reeds.

This boat is made from a tree.

This boat is powered by the wind.

This boat is powered by steam.

This boat uses paddles.

This boat uses propellers.

This boat breaks through ice.

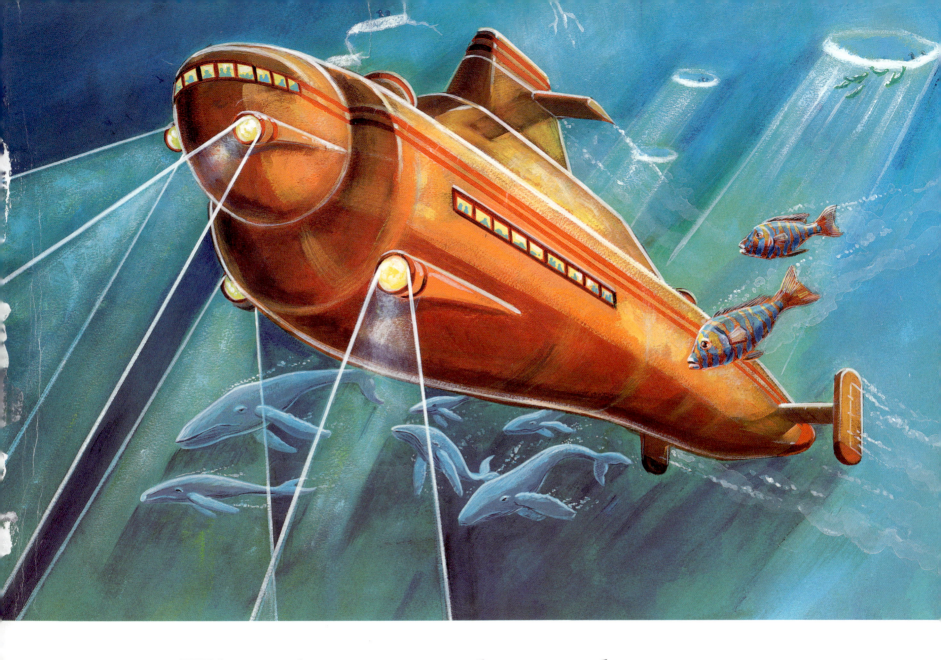

This boat sails under ice.

This boat sails under a bridge.

This boat sails on top of a bridge.

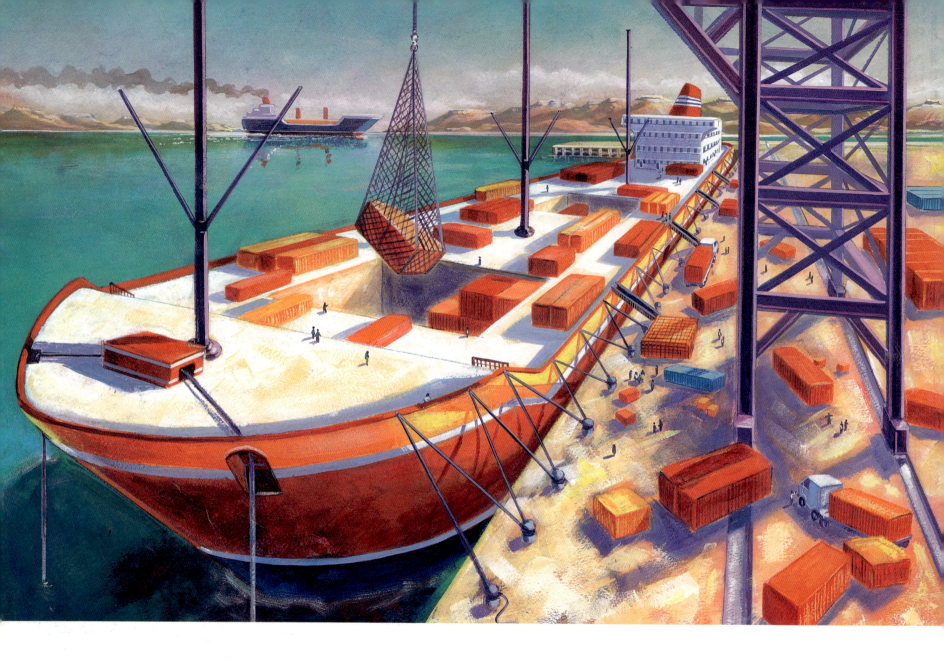

This boat carries cargo.

This boat is ready to set sail.

The USS *Holland*—
the first wholly successful submarine

Donald McKay's *Lightning* clipper

SeaCat ferry

USS *West Virginia*
Ohio-class submarine

SS *Titanic*